The fisherman

Mr Oldcastle

The old fishing boat

Gumdrop's Engine

Horace

# GUMDROP
## at Sea

*Written and illustrated by*
*Val Biro*

AWARD PUBLICATIONS LIMITED

On a sunny summer's day the road to the sea was jammed. Something was holding up the traffic and people kept beeping their horns.

"*Honk-honk*" went another horn, the brass horn of an Austin Clifton Heavy 12/4 of 1926, called Gumdrop.

Mr Josiah Oldcastle was getting impatient too, and so was his dog Horace. He went "woof-woof".

A car had broken down in front. It belonged to the
Bumblebee family, Mr Oldcastle's neighbours.

"It won't go!" complained Mr B.

"Our holiday's ruined!" wailed Mrs B.

"We want ice cream!" demanded their children.

So Mr Oldcastle drove up to
help his neighbours. They hitched
the battered car to Gumdrop for a
tow, while Mrs B directed the traffic
with her parasol.

As Gumdrop towed the heavy car to a garage, his engine began to complain with ominous *clangety* noises. Mr Oldcastle didn't like those at all.

"Your big end's going," said the garage man. This worried Mr Oldcastle, but they all wanted to get to the seaside. So the Bumblebees left their car for repair, squeezed into Gumdrop, and they continued their journey to the sea.

Struggling up a steep hill on the way, Gumdrop's engine went *clangety clang-clang*. The Bumblebees were really too heavy for the old car, and Mr Oldcastle didn't like those engine noises one little bit.

"Your big end's going!" warned Mr B.
"What a calamity!" cried Mrs B.
"We want ice cream!" moaned the kids.
"Woof-woof!" went Horace.

There, at last, was the harbour. Everybody cheered up: even the engine sounded happy. Good old Gumdrop had brought them all safely to the sea.

But suddenly those dreadful *clangety* noises began again, now worse than ever. Then, with an almighty loud BANG, the engine stopped.

"Oh my goodness!" exclaimed Mr Oldcastle. "The engine's blown up!" There was oil everywhere and a gaping hole in the crank-case. A hole that couldn't be repaired.

Gumdrop would need a new engine now. But where could he find another 1926 Austin 12/4 engine?

For the moment there was nothing to be done, so Mr Oldcastle went with the others for a sail. Poor Gumdrop was left standing on the shore.

They hired an old fishing boat. "All aboard!"
ordered Mr B, who was the captain now. "Weigh
anchor! Hoist the sails!" And they sailed away
on the tide, with many a "Gybe-oh!"
and "Ready about!"

Mrs B lay back to sunbathe under her parasol. The children ate ice cream and Horace was fishing. Everybody was happy – except Mr Oldcastle who was worrying about Gumdrop's broken engine.

The tide was flowing and the wind freshening. Mr B scanned the horizon with his telescope and gazed all around.

"Look, the water's nearly up to Gumdrop!" he said.

"Oh no!" cried Mr Oldcastle. "We must turn back at once or Gumdrop will be drowned!"

Just then Horace saw a fish. He leaned out to grab it, but unfortunately he lost his balance…

... and *splash*! fell straight into the water.
Mr Oldcastle did not hesitate – he
didn't want his dog drowned as
well, so he plunged right in
to save Horace.

Mr B didn't wait either and he leaned out to save Mr Oldcastle. The others rushed quickly to the side to save Horace. But all their weight and rushing tilted the boat so violently that…

… they all fell overboard!
   "Mayday, mayday!" boomed Mr B.
   "Help, help!" gurgled Mrs B.
   The children just screamed.
Mr Oldcastle was speechless as
their boat floated away.

Other boats soon came to rescue them. Everybody was soaking wet but safe. "Now we must rescue Gumdrop!" cried Mr Oldcastle.

The water was already up to Gumdrop's mudguards.

"Shoulders to the wheel!" commanded Mr B as everyone pushed and heaved to get the car back on dry land again.

But where was Horace? In all the confusion of getting soaked and being rescued Mr Oldcastle couldn't remember what had happened to his dog. He was truly all at sea.

Just then he heard a sort of muffled bark. It came from their fishing boat which was floating in on the tide. Mr Oldcastle scrambled on board. The odd bark came from under the engine cover. He tore it off – and there was Horace, sitting by the engine, safe and sound!

He folded the dog in his arms and felt happy for the first time that day.

Then Mr Oldcastle looked at the engine. It was big and beautiful – and it was exactly like Gumdrop's.

"A genuine 1926 Austin 12/4 engine and not a hole anywhere!" he said. He could hardly believe his luck. "You clever dog – you've found the perfect engine for Gumdrop!" And Mr Oldcastle danced around until Horace got quite dizzy.

The owner of the old fishing boat was happy to sell his engine.

"It came out of an old car just like yours," said the fisherman. "Anyway I'd rather have a modern diesel," he added.

So all was well in the end. Mr Oldcastle took the precious engine to be overhauled and then returned to finish his holiday. He bought ice cream for the children and Horace caught as much fish as he wanted. Best of all, Gumdrop has a sparkling new engine now. *Brrrm-brrrm*!

One last thing. The old
fishing boat has a new name
now. It is *Gumdrop 2*.

ISBN 1-84135-309-4

Copyright © 1983 Val Biro
This edition copyright © 2004 Val Biro

First published 1983 by Hodder and Stoughton Children's Books
This revised edition first published 2004 by Award Publications Limited,
27 Longford Street, London NW1 3DZ

Printed in Malaysia